First published in the United States of America in 1998
by **MONDO Publishing**
Published in the United Kingdom in 1998
by The Bodley Head Children's Books,
an imprint of Random House UK Ltd.

For information contact:
MONDO Publishing
One Plaza Road
Greenvale, New York 11548
Visit our web site at http://www.mondopub.com

Printed in Singapore
First Mondo Printing, May 1998
98 99 00 01 02 03 04 05   HC   9 8 7 6 5 4 3 2 1
98 99 00 01 02 03 04 05   PB   9 8 7 6 5 4 3 2 1

Library of Congress Cataloging-in-Publication Data
Prater, John.
On top of the world / John Prater.
p.   cm.
Summary: On a warm night in a moonlit playground, four toy
animals climb and climb to the top of the world and then have
the fun of coming down again.
ISBN 1-57255-649-8 (hardcover : alk. paper)
— ISBN 1-57255-650-1 (pbk. : alk. paper)
[1. Toys—Fiction.   2. Animals—Fiction.   3. Playgrounds—Fiction.]
I. Title.
PZ7.P8867On   1998
[E]—dc21   98-16344   CIP   AC

On Top of the World

JOHN PRATER

Once a year, on a
warm summer night
when the moon is full,
all toys everywhere
leave their owners
for a night of fun.

Bear, Rabbit, Mimi, and Peep felt very excited.

"I haven't done this before," said Bear.

"We haven't either," said Mimi and Peep.

"Well I have," said Rabbit, "and it's great fun!"

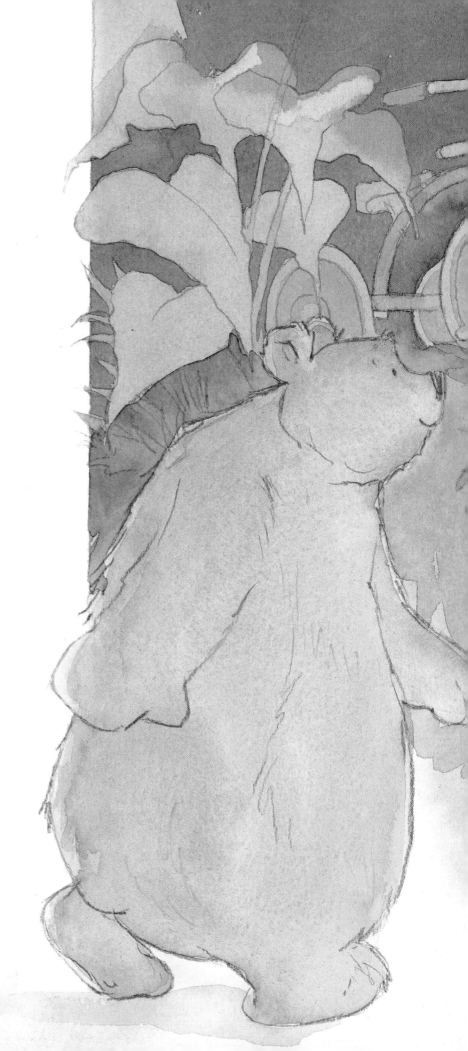

"Here we are,"
said Rabbit.

"What is it?"
asked Peep.

"It looks like
a very big step,"
said Bear.

They climbed up.

"Oh look, another one," said Mimi.

"Yes," said Rabbit. "There are many more. And when we have climbed them all we will be on top of the world."

Up and up
they climbed,

and up some more
until at last . . .

as night became day,
they found themselves
on top of the world!

"I can see forever,"
said Bear.

"Don't look down,"
said Rabbit.

"I just did," said
Peep, "and I'm
dizzy."

Mimi nearly fell,
but was saved
by the tail.

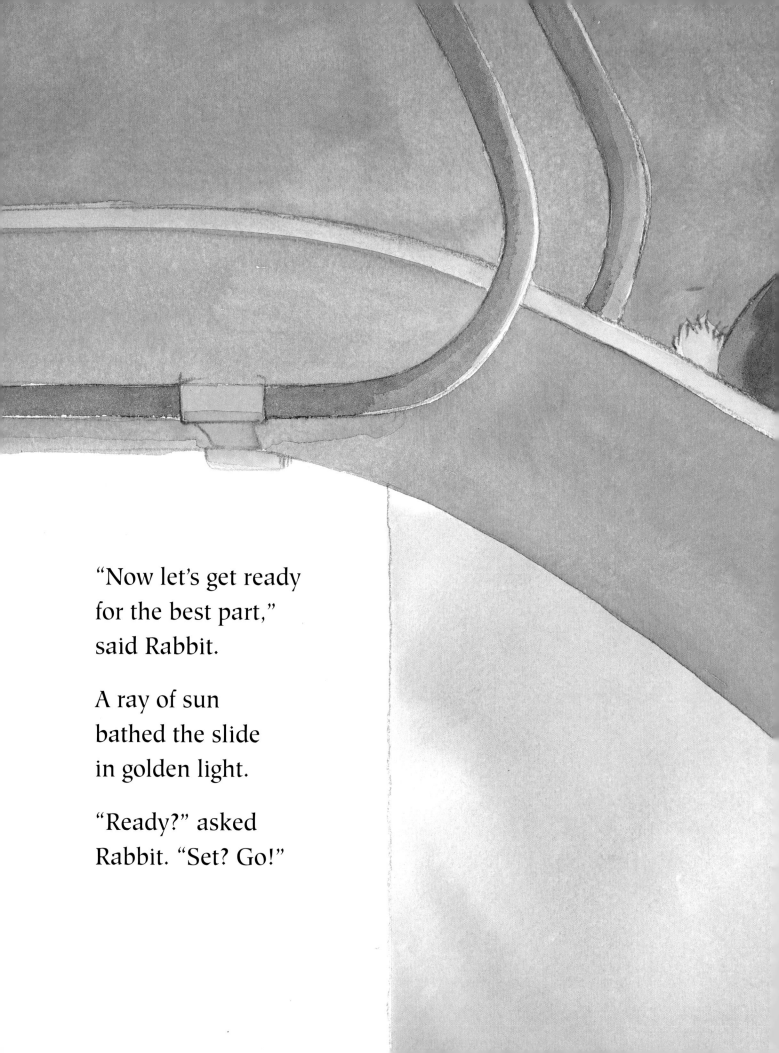

"Now let's get ready
for the best part,"
said Rabbit.

A ray of sun
bathed the slide
in golden light.

"Ready?" asked
Rabbit. "Set? Go!"

"Wow!" said Peep.
"Let's do it again."

But there wasn't
any more time.
Until next year,
when on a warm
moonlit night . . .

all toys everywhere
will leave their
owners for a night
of fun.